W9-AVK-323

This book is dedicated to my daughter Katie,
who inspired me to share her bedtime characters
and stories with other children.

www.mascotbooks.com

Hippo Pottymouth

©2016 Pottymouth Books LLC. All Rights Reserved. No part of this
publication may be reproduced, stored in a retrieval system or transmitted
in any form by any means electronic, mechanical, or photocopying,
recording or otherwise without the permission of the author.

For more information, please contact:
Mascot Books
560 Herndon Parkway #120
Herndon, VA 20170
info@mascotbooks.com

Library of Congress Control Number: 2016915450

CPSIA Code: PRT1016A
ISBN-13: 978-1-63177-892-6

Printed in the United States

HIPPO POTTYMOUTH

by Ken Lefkowitz

Illustrated by Caitlyn Notaro

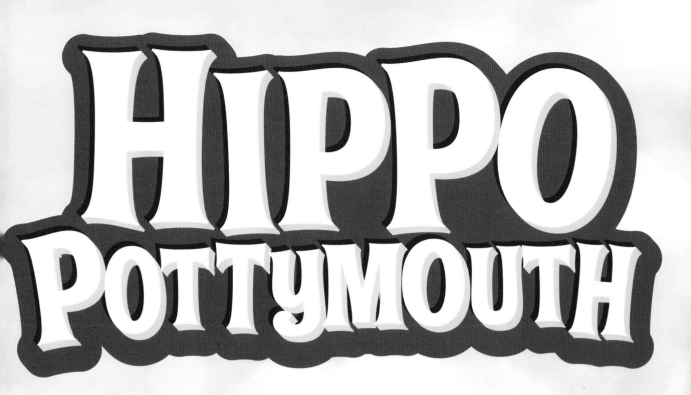

Bitty was in the middle of a daydream

while preparing a flower arrangement for Mrs. Hippo, whose family had just moved to town. Bitty knew everyone in Hill Hollow and was anxious to meet the newest Hill Hollowians.

Where are they from? What are they like? Do they have any kids my age? She couldn't stop thinking of questions!

She heard the familiar jing-a-ling of the door and felt her heart racing as she wondered if the unfamiliar voices might belong to the Hippos.

Her thoughts were interrupted by a loud thud, followed by a collection of odd new words **"BLEEEEP BLEEEEP"** that Bitty didn't recognize. She didn't know what the words meant, but she knew they made her belly feel a little sour.

Bitty swung around the counter and it was no surprise the customers didn't look familiar. In fact, Bitty had never seen animals like these before.

Even though Bitty jumped off that same stool every day without falling, this time she **tripped, tumbled,** and **bounced** into Mrs. Hippo.

"Oh! I'm sorry! You must be Mrs. Hippo! This is so exciting! I mean, I'm sorry for bouncing into you. I'm excited to meet you!"

"Who are you?" asked a small voice.

"I'm Bitty. I help my mom run the flower shop. Who are you?"

"I'm Hippi. We just moved here from Urbania. How old are you?"

"I'm six. How old are you?"

"I just turned eight," Hippi replied.

3

"**Did you fall?**" Bitty asked.

"Yeah, I tripped on the step. I banged my knee."

"It looks like you scraped it too. Do you want a bandage?"

"Sure!"

Bitty disappeared into the back room and returned with a bandage.

"Hippi, what were those words you said when you fell? I've never heard them before. **They didn't sound very nice.**"

"Oh, I'm sorry. I didn't mean to . . . they just came out," Hippi said sheepishly, realizing that Hill Hollow must be different than Urbania, where bad words were common.

After a moment Bitty jumped up. "Oooh, were they *potty* words?"

"In Urbania, where we lived before, everyone used words like that. You really weren't supposed to, but no one paid much attention. If they upset you I'll try not to use them."

Bitty and Hippi went outside to play. "So, how did you get your name, Bitty?" Hippi asked.

"My real name is Bittyanne. Since I was an itty bitty bunny, my family started calling me Bitty. Is Hippi short for—"

But Bitty's question was cut off by *those* words again. "BLEEEP BLEEEP BLEEEP!"

Bitty felt that sour feeling in her belly again, but she also felt bad for Hippi. "Ooh, that must have hurt!"

"Not too much," said Hippi. "I didn't see that branch. We didn't have many trees in Urbania."

Bitty thought for a moment. "Hippi, you have a **potty mouth!**"

"Before I moved here, everyone called me Hippo Pottymouth. I got used to it after a while."

"Can I call you Hippo Pottymouth?" asked Bitty.

"If you want to," Hippi said.

"What's that?"

"You've never seen a dandelion?" replied Bitty. "They start out as pretty yellow flowers, like that one over there. Then they become white and puffy. Grown-ups don't like them, but I think they make the grass look nicer than just plain green. After all, flowers make everything better. I think grown-ups are silly."

"They look nice to me."

Bitty held the puffy flower in front of her mouth, then took a deep breath and blew. "You just can't blow it toward Mrs. Harper's yard. Otherwise, she'll come yell at you."

Hippi thought that if Bitty's one flower looked nice, maybe a big bunch of flower puffs would look even nicer. Bitty's eyes opened wide and her jaw dropped as she realized what Hippi had in mind. "Wow! Are you going to blow all of those at once?"

"Yep," Hippi replied casually. **"Watch this!"**

Hippi held up the white puffy bouquet, took a deep breath, and blew as hard as she could, completely forgetting Bitty's warning about Mrs. Harper.

As Bitty felt the breeze tickle the tips of her ears, she realized that it was too late. They watched as the giant cloud was carried over the white picket fence, scattering millions of dandelion seeds across Mrs. Harper's perfectly manicured grass.

Mrs. Harper had been watching from her window. She came out yelling, **"What are you kids doing!?** Get away from my yard . . . you're ruining my grass!"

Bitty grabbed Hippi's arm and ran around the corner of the flower shop.

But Hippi couldn't be more excited. "Wow! Did you see that?" exclaimed Hippi. "Now that was fun!"

"**What do you mean?** She screamed at us! And once our moms find out, we're going to get in trouble."

"They won't find out," replied Hippi.

"Sure, they will. Everyone knows everything that happens in Hill Hollow."

Just then, Mrs. Harper caught up to them. Bitty and Hippi just stared at Mrs. Harper in shock, and Hippi exclaimed, **"Oh, BLEEEP."**

Mrs. Harper's mouth dropped. She stared at Hippi and said, "You have quite a foul mouth! Didn't your parents teach you not to use bad words? I don't know where you are from but we don't like language like that." She was so stunned by Hippi's potty words that she completely forgot about the dandelion incident. "...and you, Bitty! What would your mother say if she knew you were spending your time with someone who has such a potty mouth?!"

Mrs. Harper turned and walked away. Bitty was embarrassed. Her ears drooped down and she felt ashamed. **Hippi then realized** that Hill Hollow really was a different sort of place, just like Bitty had said. And she understood that she might have just gotten Bitty into trouble.

Hippi then explained, "Urbania was a big city. My brother and sister and I could have lots of fun without Mom and Dad finding out. And no one really bothered us about our words. As long as we did well in class and didn't get into too much trouble, we could do what we wanted."

"*That* will change now. You'll see," Bitty replied.

A moment passed and Bitty continued, "I'll make you a deal. I'll try to help you stay out of trouble."

"What do I have to do?" asked Hippi.

"You have to try too."

"It's a deal!"

Bitty was glad to have a new friend to play with. And while Hippi had been nervous about moving to a new town, Hill Hollow seemed like a pretty fun place. The summer was just getting started and the new friends were looking forward to all of the adventures they would have together.

About the Author

Ken Lefkowitz lives in central New Jersey with his wife Tracy, daughter Katie, and their assorted furry friends. Katie's bedtime stories always include her best plush friends. When it was time to teach Katie about pottymouth language, her purple hippopotamus named Hippi was the perfect inspiration for *Hippo Pottymouth*. Katie's hysterical and uncontrollable laughter inspired this book.